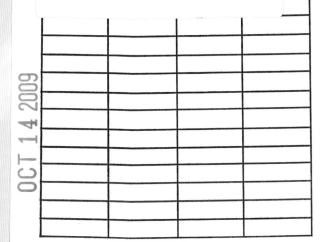

For my parents, Stephen and Bernice, who always take the time to
hear what I'm really saying—even now. Thank you for listening. —C.D.

To Maddie, with much love. —R.B.

Text copyright © 2009 by Christin Ditchfield. Illustrations copyright © 2009 by Rosalind Beardshaw.
All rights reserved. Published in the United States by Golden Books, an imprint of Random House Children's
Books, a division of Random House, Inc., 1745 Broadway, New York, NY 10019. Golden Books,
A Golden Book, and the G colophon are registered trademarks of Random House, Inc.
www.goldenbooks.com
www.randomhouse.com/kids
Educators and librarians, for a variety of teaching tools, visit us at
www.randomhouse.com/teachers
Library of Congress Control Number: 2008923774
ISBN: 978-0-375-84181-1 (trade) — ISBN: 978-0-375-94351-5 (lib. bdg.)
PRINTED IN CHINA
10 9 8 7 6 5 4 3 2 1
First Edition

"Shwatsit!"

no one knows just what it means

By Christin Ditchfield

Illustrated by Rosalind Beardshaw

A GOLDEN BOOK · NEW YORK

Our baby has a favorite word—
The silliest word you've ever heard . . .

"Shwatsit!"

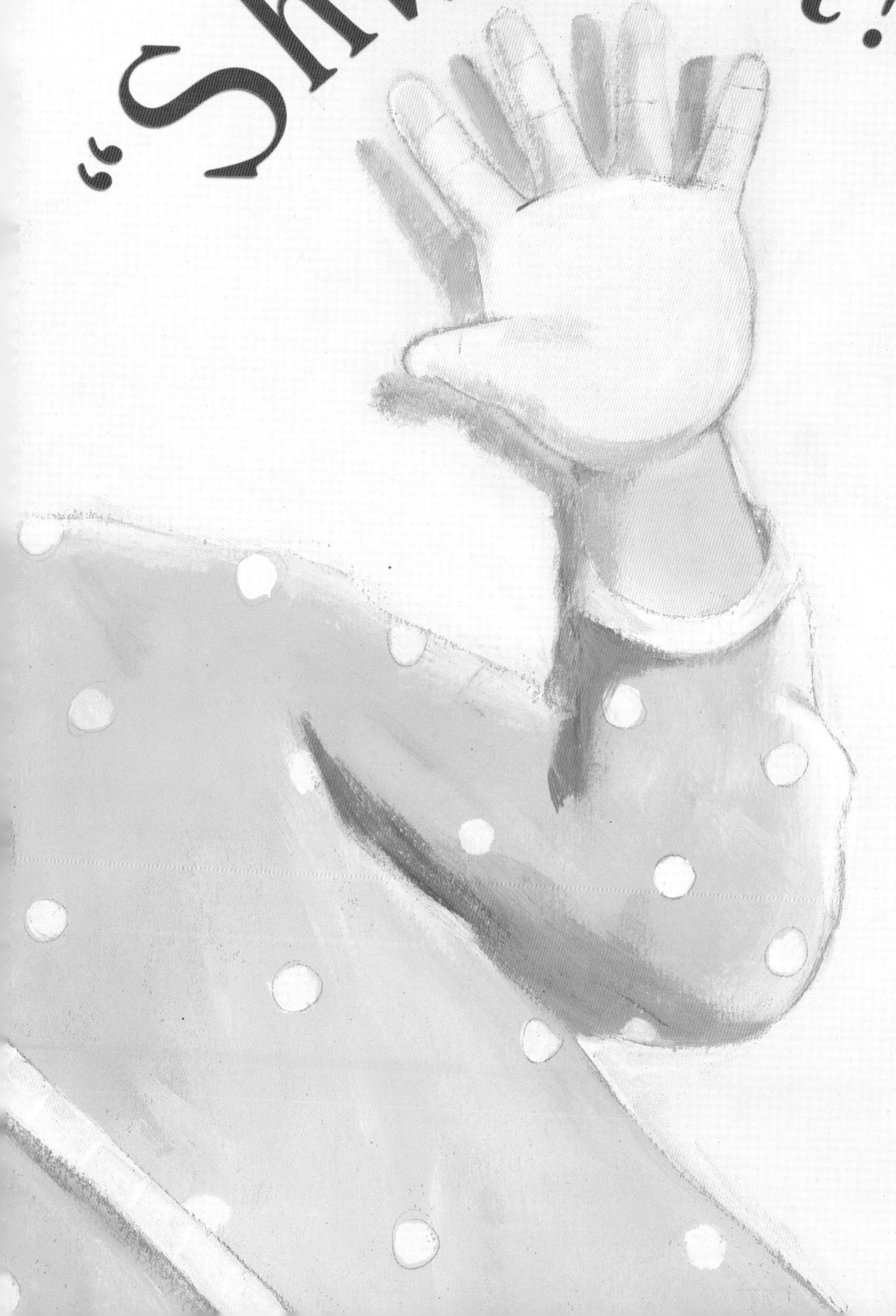

No one knows just
what it means.
It could be "eggs" or
"toast" or "beans."

"Shwatsit!"

It could be "backpack," "bus," or "Joe."

It could be "brush" or "hair" or "bow."

"Shwatsit!"

Is *shwatsit* "store" or "car" or "gas"?

"Shwatsit!"

Or "bird" or "sky" or "cloud" or "grass"?

It could be "kite," "balloon," or "string."
It could be "sandbox," "slide," or "swing."

"Shwatsit" this and "shwatsit" that!

"Shwatsit!"

"Shwatsit" dog and "shwatsit" cat!

"Shwatsit" book and "shwatsit" brother!

"Shwatsit" father? "Shwatsit" mother?

"Shwatsit" washer, "shwatsit" dryer.

"Shwatsit!"

"Shwatsit!"

"Shwatsit" stairs climb higher, higher. . . .

It could be "clothes" or "laundry basket."
Hear her ask . . . and ask . . . and ask it?

"Shwatsit!"

"Wait a minute! Hold
it there. . . .
    "She wants it, Mom.
She wants her bear!"

"Shwatsit!"

Say it fast: "Shwatsit!"

"Shwatsit!"

Aha! At last!
Shwatsit is "She wants it!"—fast!

"Shwatsit!"

Baby's word sure means a lot.

"Shwatsit!"

She's such a clever little tot!